It's Not All Black and White It's No
Not All Black and White It's
White It's Not All Black and
Black and White It's Not All
It's Not All Black and White
and White

It's Not All
Black and White It's
White It's Not All Black and
Black and White

Multiracial Youth
Speak Out

St. Stephen's Community House

Not All Black
White It's Not All Black and
Black and White It's Not All
It's Not All Black and White
and White It's Not All Black
Not All Black and White It's
White It's Not All Black and
Black and White It's Not All
It's Not All Black and White
and White It's Not All Black
Not All Black and White It's
White It's Not All Black and

annick press
toronto + new york + vancouver

© 2012 St. Stephen's Community House (text)
Edited by Andrea Douglas
Designed by Monica Charny
Cover art and design by victoR gad
All photographs and original artwork provided by members and family of the
Making Sense of One group, St. Stephen's Community House, Toronto, Ontario, Canada
Frames used throughout, © Nicemonkey, © Luba V Nel, © Balint Radu, © Yellowdesignstudio,
© Aliaksey Hintau, © Michael Mcdonald; 25 grunge paper texture, © Roxana González;
64–65 spheres, © Anna Rassadnikova; 66 ice cream cones, © Kheng Guan Toh; 68 corrugated
cardboard with torn edges, © Martijn Mulder; 89 black spot grunge, © Sergey Denisov;
95 clipped paper, © Natalie Shmeleva; 104–107 corkboard background, © MorganOliver;
104–107 note paper, © Picsfive: all © Dreamstime.com
The excerpt from "itty bitty" on pp. 51–55 was originally published, in slightly different form,
as part of a full-length play in *Other Tongues: Mixed-Race Women Speak Out*, Inanna
Publications, Toronto, Canada, 2010. Reprinted here by permission.

Annick Press Ltd.

We acknowledge the support of the Canada Council for the Arts, the Ontario Arts Council,
and the Government of Canada through the Canada Book Fund (CBF) for our publishing
activities.

ONTARIO ARTS COUNCIL
CONSEIL DES ARTS DE L'ONTARIO

Cataloging in Publication

It's not all black and white : multiracial youth speak out / St. Stephen's
Community House.

ISBN 978-1-55451-380-2

1. Racially mixed people—Race identity—Canada—Juvenile literature.
2. Racially mixed people—Canada—Attitudes—Juvenile literature.
3. Racially mixed people—Canada—Interviews—Juvenile literature.
4. Racially mixed people—Canada—Biography—Juvenile literature.
5. Minority youth—Canada—Juvenile literature. 6. Prejudices—Canada—
Juvenile literature. 7. Self-esteem—Juvenile literature. I. St. Stephen's
Community House (Toronto, Ont.) II. Title: It is not all black and white.

FC106.R33I85 2012   j305.800971   C2012-901086-3

Distributed in Canada by:
Firefly Books Ltd.
66 Leek Crescent
Richmond Hill, ON
L4B 1H1

Published in the U.S.A. by
Annick Press (U.S.) Ltd.

Distributed in the U.S.A. by:
Firefly Books (U.S.) Inc.
P.O. Box 1338
Ellicott Station
Buffalo, NY 14205

Printed in Canada

MIX
Paper from
responsible sources
FSC
www.fsc.org
FSC® C004071

Visit us at: www.annickpress.com
Visit St. Stephen's Community House at: www.ststephenshouse.com
Visit victoR gad at: www.victorgad.com

Contents

Preface

"Wow, what good hair you have!"

"Such a beautiful complexion! You are so exotic."

"Are you mixed? What is your background?"

These are the types of reactions I have elicited since I was a child, and they continue today. I am West Indian, French Armenian, and Canadian, so it is not surprising that people want to figure out who I am.

My biracial journey began at the nursery with a confused father looking for a brown kid. My dad was surprised to find a very light—almost white—baby with straight, black hair. It was a different time, when interracial relationships were not as accepted and mixed-race kids were few. As a kid, I didn't understand the complexity of race or the labels "mulatto," "half-breed," or "mixed." I simply knew that my mom was white and my dad was black.

In my teenage years, I would switch from trying to be "more black" to chilling with all white folks. I forgot I held black history and culture. I lived for years thinking that I was a white girl. It took a long time, but I finally embraced my black heritage. I now realize being biracial is a gift of strength, wisdom, and heightened awareness. I went through this confusing process in silence, but luckily you don't have to.

It is thanks to St. Stephen's Community House's recognition of the increase in numbers of mixed-race youth and the importance of race and racial issues that this book is available.

St. Stephen's Community House is a unique, community-based social service agency that has been serving the needs of Kensington

Market and surrounding neighborhoods in downtown West Toronto since 1962.

I was privileged to begin working with St. Stephen's Community House, Youth Department, many years ago. I recently became aware of a particular need for a focus on questions of racial identity, especially around being of mixed race, and so the project called Making Sense of One was created.

I coordinated the project, which involved a group of phenomenal and wise youth who opened up and shared their stories, ultimately to create this book. In line with the Youth Department's philosophy that young people should be encouraged to think critically about themselves and the world around them, the book addresses key issues that affect multiracial youth as the experts of their own lives. It is St. Stephen's third book for youth published with Annick Press. The first two are books about teen sexuality: *The Little Black Book for Girlz* and *The Little Black Book for Guys*.

It is our hope that you will find some connection to the stories presented here and that they will encourage conversations about race. The ultimate goal is that one day we will look beyond race—to come to an acceptance of people regardless of our differences. Until then, this multicultural world requires us to maneuver among racial boxes. So while we wait for further change to occur, we hope that this book will help guide you. We know that these issues are complex and that this book may not cover all the topics connected to being of mixed race, but it is a good start. Journey with us.

—*Karen Arthurton*
Coordinator, Making Sense of One
St. Stephen's Community House, Youth Department

The Making Sense of One group: (top row, from left) Ialo Iorza, Yvonne Sanchez-Tieu, Kalale Dalton, Chiloh Turner, Bianca Craven, Janine Berridge; (bottom row, from left) Elizabeth Jennifer Hollo, Karuna Sagara, Karen Arthurton   Absent: Bailey Allett, Andrew Ernest Brankley, Justin Robinson

INTRODUCTION

Yes, we made it! In 2010, a group of eleven young people began meeting at our community youth drop-in center on a weekly basis to talk about the one thing that we all had in common: being of mixed race. During this process, we also welcomed a number of new faces who donated their time to talk about race.

This local drop-in center, better known as the Youth Arcade, became a second home to many of us. Our group leader often spoke about the issues around being of mixed race, and we discovered this was something that we could all relate to, regardless of our ages.

It wasn't an issue we thought about on a day-to-day basis, but after our discussions it was becoming increasingly clear that not only our group but also many like us have unique experiences and understandings of what it means to be multiracial. The interaction of two or more races comes with assets and privileges but also sometimes with feelings of confusion, anger, resentment, isolation, or rejection. We needed a positive space to experience and express our feelings, so we talked, we laughed, we argued, we cried, and we created this fantastic book, which reflects many of our conversations.

In this book you'll find a collection of personal stories, poetry, and artwork by a group of nearly twenty mixed-race youth. There are also interviews based on the experiences of those who are either mixed race and/or raising mixed-race children. We have also included the voices of several insightful mentors of older generations who have passed on their wisdom to us, and now to you. We hope you will find answers, gain insight, feel connected, and ultimately be inspired by our stories.

So read on, friends, read on ...

—*The Making Sense of One group*

RACE

What is *race*, anyway? There doesn't appear to be just one answer to this question. Some say that there are four races: black, white, red, and yellow. Others say that there are many: white, black, Asian, Aboriginal, or Hawaiian, for instance. Race has been used to classify humans according to their common ancestry, using physical characteristics such as skin color, stature, hair texture, and facial features as visible definers. Race is also used to describe a group of people who share some biological characteristics and who differ from other groups because of these characteristics. Still others say that there is no such thing as race, and that race was socially constructed to create divisions among groups. Even though its definition is not completely clear, race plays an important part in everyone's life, as does racism.

MIXED RACE

Mixed race is a broad term used to describe people whose ancestries come from multiple races. *Biracial* refers specifically to people with only two different races in their heritage (e.g., black and white). *Multiracial* refers specifically to people with two or more races (e.g., white, black, and Native American).

RACE VS CULTURE

Race is based on your physical and/or biological characteristics. *Culture* consists of the social aspects shared by a group of people, such as beliefs, religion, art, food, music, and so on. While a person can change and adapt his or her culture over time, his or her race(s) cannot change.

**Changing past,
constant future.
The two rivers join ...**

I view my future as being constant, because
even though I am from two different cultures,
I always picture a future that combines both—
my two cultural and racial backgrounds flowing
into one stream.

—Spencer Brigham

CHAPTER 1
We've Come a Long Way

So it is 2012, and we would like to believe that the world is free of racism, discrimination, and hate. All should be good now, but sadly, this is not the case. Although we have come a long way from the days when mixed-race relationships were taboo (and, in some places, illegal) and mixed-race folks were excluded, we still experience some challenges. Issues such as racism, stereotyping, and feelings of being unaccepted by friends and family continue to affect some mixed-race youth. In all this confusion, we are trying to make sense of how it's not all black and white: we explore race, culture, and ways to belong. In this chapter, you will hear from different generations of mixed-race people. Using poetry, testimonials, and interviews they will discuss what it means to be multiracial or to raise multiracial children. Join us as we uncover the first steps to finding our way home.

ra·cism – noun – a belief in the superiority of a particular race – prejudice based on this – lack of empathy toward other races, especially as a result of this prejudice – discrimination can be based on differences in skin color, complexion, hair type, and so on

ONE OF MANY

MANY MANY MANY MANY MANY MANY MANY MANY

lalo lorza

Many people assume that children born mixed race grow up to be confused, lost, and isolated. This is true for some, but for others being mixed leads to exploration. Knowing where you come from helps you decide where you may want to go and unlocks mysteries long forgotten or kept secret.

Racism and oppression still thrive in the present, and mixed-race people are not excluded from racism. In fact, being mixed generally adds even more challenges, such as guilt, self-hate, and pressure to fit in. Even in the multicultural environment that many grew up with, mixed-race people may face discrimination from all sides and all angles.

We live in a world where people often categorize each other based on skin color and features. How can someone of two or more races feel comfortable in a single box when parts of who they are don't fit? The reality is that it's time for nonmixed people and systems to stop trying to fit us into racial categories and just accept the fact that we are not one race but many—or, as I like to say, we are many races that create ONE.

STOP trying to fit us in

Race Is Ubiquitous

Elizabeth Jennifer Hollo

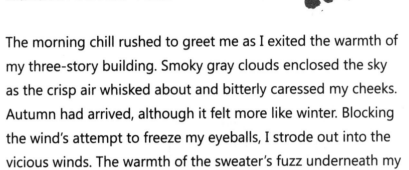

The morning chill rushed to greet me as I exited the warmth of my three-story building. Smoky gray clouds enclosed the sky as the crisp air whisked about and bitterly caressed my cheeks. Autumn had arrived, although it felt more like winter. Blocking the wind's attempt to freeze my eyeballs, I strode out into the vicious winds. The warmth of the sweater's fuzz underneath my jacket made me feel snug, like sitting on a fur carpet in front of a fire in the dead of winter.

I had left early that Saturday morning to go to Hungarian school—by myself. It was a blessing from above; being independent made me feel more like a woman, like I was growing up. I had gotten up and gotten ready quickly, while my mother and father were still fast asleep. I made as little noise as I possibly could, then I woke my father up when I was finished.

"Daddy, I'm going to school!"

He sat up briskly, fetched his oversized glasses from the table, and looked me up and down.

"I won't make it on time if you come, Papa. You should stay and go back to sleep."

He smiled slightly, reached over to grab his wallet, and pulled out two bus tickets. I took them with a grin and kissed him while falling onto his neck for a hug. Somehow I knew he understood.

The chilly air meant nothing against the warmth of my clothing. My mind was weaving in and out of the nature around me: the colors of the changing leaves, the crunching sound the dry ones made as I treaded heavily through the field. I looked up at the rain clouds above me as it began to drizzle. Contentment set in as I felt the relief of the clouds releasing their moisture onto the earth. Feeling magnificent, feeling mature, feeling blissful and blessed. Who knew it could be wrenched away so fast?

Dressed in pink, old, and gray, I'd have
never thought of her that way.
Didn't know her from anywhere; she just
came near.
She grimaced at me and winced away.
"Nigger," she whispered. "Filthy," she
sneered.
My heart skipped a beat.
My blood began to curl.
The world stopped moving.
"Nigger!" she screamed.
"You're a criminal!" she said.
My face boiled up. I swear I turned red!
Shocked, infuriated, heartbroken, and in
tears.
Confused and frustrated, not knowing
what to do.
"What?" I cried, as she cringed away.
"You filthy nigger!" she screeched, hurrying
her pace.

"What did I do?" I squealed after her,
trying to catch up.
She turned to me, her eyes threatening
my every move.
Stopped in my tracks; wounded to the
core.
She turned and ran, swearing at me.
I watched her go, watched her scream.
Wondering, why me?

Until that day I never really knew what racism was or what effect it could have on you. When I experienced it in elementary school I didn't understand, but as I stood there—heart icy as snow, blood past boiling point, mind in chaos, and feeling vulnerable—I became aware that racism is everywhere. It can strike at any time, and I have to be aware that race is a huge part of life, especially for a woman of color. Horrendous and remarkable all at once, race is ubiquitous.

IT'S 2012, WHERE HAVE YOU BEEN?

Bianca Craven

Black, white, and everything in-between
Racism, you thought you could go unseen
It's 2012, where have you been?
A thing of the past, 1918
When I was a kid, I thought I was black
Used to have my hair in braids, cornrows to the back
Played jump rope 'n' hopscotch, never stepped on a crack
I was just a kid, hangman and tic tac
Then high school came, like "oh my gosh"
I'll never forget the first time I was called "whitewash"
It was by this white chick who thought she was hot
I kicked her right in her gut for talking her talk
That was the first fight of many to come
Are you white? Are you black? They'd all gather 'round
That word I don't like, I just don't like the sound
"Nigga," that's what some white people say when I'm not around
I heard it again and it came from a friend
It hurts me to hear, and she says it again
Black, white, and everything in-between
Just don't say the *N* word, you got it? Seen?
Well that's what I thought, you know what I mean
I keep hearing my own people say it, they say it to me
Black, white, and everything in between
They all say the *N* word, so it seems
It's 2012, where have you been?
Racism a thing of the past, 1993
We have come a long way, far too far
For us to still be calling each other "Nigga"
Black, white, and everything in between
Let's all become one, now dat would be sweet!

interview with carol camper

PART ONE

Yvonne Sanchez-Tieu

Carol Camper is the editor of *Miscegenation Blues: Voices of Mixed Race Women*, an anthology of writing that includes the voices of more than forty mixed-race women.

Q Tell me about your racial/ethnic background.

a I come from a background of mixing Caucasian, black, and Native American. I know my father is a white man; my mother is black but she has Native American ancestry as well.

Q When did you first realize that there was a difference between you and the majority of people around you?

a Well, I began to realize that when I was about eight. It coincided with moving to a larger town from a small community, so there were more people around, more interactions, a bigger school, that kind of thing. It came up because of name-calling. People started to call me "nigger," and I didn't really know what they meant at first. Later on I figured that piece out, but the older I got, the more aware I was of differences between me and the rest of my community.

Q What are some of the biggest challenges that you have experienced or faced as a mixed-race woman?

The biggest challenge has been racism. In my childhood, not everyone could tell that I was black, but it was clear to most that I was not white, or not their idea of white. My non-whiteness was a big problem in my community. When people figured out or heard about who I actually was (or the part that counted, anyway), then I became a definite target. The questions about my identity stopped, and the aggression began. So you know I had the full gamut of experiences—name-calling, violence, lost opportunities because of racism.

How did you deal with those difficult circumstances?

i WAS NOT THEIR IDEA OF WHITE

A lot of people don't understand that it's much easier to understand more obvious types of racism. Often, people of color will feel the insult but they might not be able to clearly describe what the problem is. This can be more damaging than more obvious forms of racism because it affects how you feel inside. It is also harder to challenge, and it becomes very difficult to believe your gut instinct if you have felt insulted but you can't even explain why.

How is it, raising a child as a mixed-race mother? Are there any challenges? Did you talk to your child about race? Do you think it is important to?

Yeah, I think it is important. I grew up in a family that didn't talk about race despite the fact that among us there were different races and the topic was going to come up.

The man I married and the father of my children is a white man, and so my children are mixed with more white, and they are much fairer than I am. And I thought it might come up that they might pass for white to a lot of people but I didn't want them to pass. I wanted them to be proud of their African heritage, their Native American heritage.

I have asked them periodically how they identify, and one time my son said "white," and you know, I didn't argue with him. I just was like, "Hmm, okay we'll work on that." And other times he said "mixed." And my daughter usually says "mixed," and people have identified them as such—you know, people at their school, people at the community—they have said "Are you mixed?" that kind of thing, and so they do get it reflected back from the community that they're not entirely white. But for the most part, the regular white guy on the street doesn't really know that about them.

ARE YOU MIXED?

WHAT AM I SUPPOSED TO LOOK LIKE?

Leslie Kachena McCue

I remember taking a cab to work early one morning. I was working with a Native traditional performing arts organization where I performed traditional stories and dances that I've known all my life. The cab driver asked me where I was going, and when I told him, he said, "Are you sure you want to go there?" Of course I do, I thought; I need to get to work just like everyone else. I brushed off the odd comment, and we continued to my destination.

We arrived at my workplace, but the cab driver told me to wait in the cab a minute because there was a dangerous person standing by the entrance. Confused, I looked

In·di·an — noun — a member of the Aboriginal peoples of North and South America (other than the Inuit and Métis) or their descendants — the use of this term has declined because it reflects Christopher Columbus's mistaken idea, while seeking Asia in 1492, that he had landed in the East Indies; he called the people he encountered "Indios," which was not only inaccurate but also falsely implied there was a racial or cultural unity across all the Aboriginal peoples of the Americas — many now consider the term to be obsolete and even offensive — the term may be used among Aboriginal peoples, however, partially because it is embedded in legislation that is still in effect — widely acceptable alternative terms are *Aboriginal peoples, Native Americans, First Nations,* and *Indigenous peoples*

out the window, only to see my co-worker. I told the cab driver it was all right and that we worked together. He just looked at me, shocked: "You work with Indians?" I told him that I work for a Native world-renowned company known for our performing talents, beautiful regalia, and entrancing music, and that I was sorry he didn't understand. "Why would you work there? You're not Native," he told me.

It was shocking to me that he would ever say such a thing, and that things like this still happen. "What is a 'Native' supposed to look like?" I asked.

He looked at me with a peculiar smile and said, "Dark hair, dark skin, and dark eyes; you're definitely white." I slammed the car door. Up until that point, I never doubted who I was and what I believed. Do hair, skin, and eye color really define a person, or is it their rich identity, teachings, stories, and their connection to mother earth? I believe there is more to me than just the color of my complexion and eyes, despite what others might think.

Although it was upsetting that something like this had to happen, it was also empowering. I know who I am and I'm proud of it. I may be biracial but I will not be defined by anyone's standards but my own.

WHEN YOUR HISTORY'S A MYSTERY

lalo lorza

I was born to a mother of Irish and Scottish descent and a father of Colombian descent. Throughout my childhood I grew up believing that I was completely white, and no one talked to me about race. Once I realized that my father didn't have white skin and that I was darker than the other white kids I grew up with, I was interested in learning the history of my father's country, and beyond that, his continent. I was very confused about my heritage because I knew that my father spoke Spanish and that Spain was in Europe, but he wasn't European and he wasn't white-skinned.

Through doing some historical research and questioning some of my family members, I learned that my father did not fall under just one ethnic category, but many. I came to the realization that the region now known as the country of

mes·ti·zo – noun – Spanish, ultimately from Latin *mixtus* (past participle of *miscere*, "to mix") – a person of mixed ancestry – in Latin and South America, the offspring of a European and an Indigenous American – during the Spanish empire's control of their American colonies (from approximately the late fifteenth century to the late nineteenth century), mestizos had fewer rights than people borne of two European parents but more rights than "Indios" or "Negros" had

Colombia had been a victim of colonization and that Spanish culture had been imposed on both the Indigenous peoples and people transported there as slaves. Thus, many people who are born in Colombia today are born to families of Native, Spanish, and African descent. Along with the majority of Colombians, my family is mestizo, which is a word created by the Spanish colonizers to describe the offspring of Spanish and Amerindian parents. Colombian culture is a combination of Spanish, African, and Indigenous traditions. Many of the foods we eat, the music we listen to, and our religious ceremonies incorporate aspects of each race.

Once I learned this, I became very interested in my Indigenous ancestry. This is because I realized that my family was in denial or uninterested in its Native roots and I believed, and still do, that this is due to the class system designed by the Spanish to create levels of hierarchy among the people. In other words: a forced assimilation into Euro-centric culture. Many of the mixed people grew accustomed—or, as I like to put it, were forced—to forget and deny their Indigenous roots. In my opinion, it was a form of cultural genocide that did not require the deaths and massacres of entire nations, although that was also going on—and still is.

Because of the history of Colombia and the injustices done to my ancestors, I feel that I would be a sell-out if I didn't acknowledge my Indigenous and African roots. In this century I have the liberty of being proud of who I am and where I come from without having to worry about being treated differently.

interview with Jorge lozano

lalo lorza

Jorge is originally from Colombia. In the early 1970s he came to Canada to escape poverty and start a new life. Jorge pursued a career in filmmaking while raising his son, lalo. Jorge has recently received a master's degree in media arts. Lalo sat down with his father to ask him about his life …

MY FATHER

Q What is our family's ethnic background?

a We don't really know much about it. But most likely we have Spanish, Native, and perhaps some black ancestry.

Q How do you identify yourself racially?

a South American mixed.

Q What was it like growing up in Colombia with a mixed-race background?

a It's normal; most people are mixed. When I grew up, there was more discrimination toward Native and black races. The people in power, the rich people, were white. I looked closer to them, so that worked in my favor.

Q What are the racial makeups of people in Colombia?

a Native, African, and Spanish. There are also people from Germany, Japan, Italy, Portugal, and other countries, who came after the Second World War and possibly before.

i feel proud that my son is mixed

Q In your experience, what is the general attitude toward people in interracial marriages in Colombia?

a It is very common and much stronger now. We are mixed and remixed.

Q How would you describe racism in Colombia?

a Racism is the same everywhere. It is a product of ignorance, social and political control, and economic power. Since 1492, it has been leveled against blacks and Natives.

Q What are some of the positive things about being of mixed race?

a It is easier to find others to be as important and as beautiful as you.

Q How was your experience raising a biracial and bicultural child?

a I respect all cultures and believe all cultures are equally important. I feel proud that my son is mixed. He has great cultural tradition in his Latino and Anglo heritage. And he cultivates the best of both and leaves the bad out.

Places, Everyone ... ACTION

Janine Berridge

I step onto a theater stage every day at around 10:00 a.m.
I play the same part
But you, a different character ... same lines that show me
    that the world around me
Seems to have a serious racial obsession ...
This was once the fuel for my self-depression
Depression of my have not's, have's, and maybe's
The fuel for yours is, is not's, and crazy
Crazy ideas of what I might be, what I am not, what I
    should be, could be, am
Recite the line, lady: "With your look, exotic, you must come
    from afar."
From lands that serve the white man's desires that cater
    to your every need
Your thoughts enslave me and bring me to my knees
Knock me down and have me lying on my face
As your eyes and questions rape me till I have no energy
    to get up and flee
For too long I have felt this way and for a while I took
    shelter in a safe haven
Where the world's racial poison could not taint me
Now I am strong and I welcome your sexual question pursuit
I welcome your questions about my "background," which, lost
    in translation, means
"What race are you?" as I can tell my answers bring you
    back to your last

Tropical West Indian, raping-all-that-the-Caribbean-is-worth
    vacation ... makes me laugh
Laugh inside at your ignorance, stupidity, childish thoughts,
    and most commonly held
Belief about what people from the Caribbean look like ...
As your common script continues to tell me that what you
    are saying translates to
"All people from the Caribbean are black Jamaicans."
Oh the lines fly out: left, right, and center
Somebody gimme a damn censor
So I can shut you the fuck up! Please let me out of this
    damn play ... 'cause really it's
The end of my day.
But no, you go on to educate me about how I can't be
    Jamaican when I haven't even
Told you what I was ... all I said was I come from West Indian
    ancestry.
This is where my insides curl with anger, but at the same
    time burst with laughter ...
Just when I think it's over, the grand finish is upon us ....
So what exactly do your parents look like?
This is where my heart starts to beat faster and my soul
    begins to speak to my mind
And tell me it will all be fine ...
But it don't matter what I say 'cause I will play this part
    once again
Tonight at around 9:00.

BY ANONYMOUS, A SIXTEEN-YEAR-OLD INDIGENOUS YOUTH

Ocean Windsong

Throughout my short life, I have been discriminated against in three different ways. I have been called "white trash," a "dirty Native," and a "half-breed." This makes me think that the world is not as accepting as I had once perceived. As a young kid, I felt like everyone accepted me for who I was. When I became older, the other kids would make fun of my nationality— that I was not good enough to be white or Native. I have grown a tolerance toward being discriminated against. Once I had stopped giving reactions to being discriminated against, it slowly died down. But being in those moments where I

half-breed – noun, adjective – offensive; a person of mixed race, especially someone of Indigenous North American and European descent

could see the sheer hatred toward me, just because of my nationality, made me worried about other people in even worse situations. Being robbed, yelled at, beaten up, and even killed. Once I moved to Toronto, one of the most multicultural cities in the world, there was absolutely zero racial discrimination toward me personally. I cannot speak for anybody else. Being in Toronto makes me feel accepted by everyone, but knowing that there is potential for such hatred toward people just solely based on the color of their skin, also makes me want to show everyone that you can't make assumptions about someone's personality based on their race.

tolerance

zero
discrimination

you can't make assumptions

Interview with Jacqueline Kalaidjian

Karuna Sagara

Jacqueline Kalaidjian is of Armenian and French background and came to Canada in 1952. Her parents were originally from Istanbul; her father was orphaned as a child because of the Armenian massacre. Her parents met and married in Paris, France. Months after her sixteenth birthday, Jacqueline's family—her grandmother, father, mother, and all five children—came to Canada so that they could start a new life.

Jacqueline sat down to talk with me about her experience of marrying outside her race and what it was like to raise two mixed-raced children in the 1960s when mixed marriages were not understood by many people.

Q How did you and your husband meet?

A In the old days, behind the art gallery, they closed the street, and there used to be a street dance, and that's where I met him, through a friend. We started talking and seeing each other, very casual, and it was all sort of hidden, and we just got a little closer and then one day, lo and behold. By then I'm working. I'm like twenty-one, twenty-two. You know, sometimes you get this weird feeling all day that something is going to happen? I went home late somehow only to find out his mother and grandmother had gone to see my parents. I don't know how they found out. Can you imagine these two dark, dark, dark, blue-black people going to see these little, little white people that don't understand English? And then of course it was a big war, and my father said, "Cannot do."

Q You couldn't see him?

a Right. It was the '50s and on top of that they were Armenian; they stick together. You stay within your own people. Then my father didn't talk to me for days. And I said, "Okay, I won't see him." And I didn't, and we started writing letters, and you know what it's like. If they had only left us alone … The more

The more you tell somebody "Don't," the more they're gonna do it.

you tell somebody "Don't," the more they're gonna do it. I'm sure if they had left us alone, well, my daughter Karen wouldn't be here. But I said, "Okay, I won't see him," and we started writing letters, and then time goes by, and by then I'm telling my parents I have a job out of town.

Q But that was a lie?

a I lived right up by Honest Ed's [a department store in a densely populated urban neighborhood]. I took one room. Now meanwhile, I had nervous breakdowns because I didn't want to make my parents unhappy, but I still wanted to see the guy. And in those days, you figure if you're with someone long enough you feel you have to get married. Somehow it seemed natural that we get married.

Q What was the general attitude toward interracial marriage when you were growing up?

a You didn't hold hands, and if you did you were looked down on. Well, black was like, forget it. I mean look at the black celebrities, even they couldn't use the same bathroom. Don't forget in the '50s it was a no-no. In the mid-1960s, it was opening up a little bit. I mean, you were still looked down on, but it wasn't as forbidden as it was in the '50s. It was still not so good.

Q Did you have to stop talking to your friends, or did they stop talking to you?

a Well, pretty well from the time I met him I had no friends, because all we did was walk the streets—walk here, walk there, go see a movie once a week. And of course, still no parents. My sister, everybody, disowned me. It took them a while before they found out that we were married. I don't know how they found out, but I guess they did. So that was that, I was disowned by everybody. By the time they met my daughter Karen, she was four years old.

disOWNed
FORBIDDEN
hidden

Q What do you think your kids thought about being mixed?

a I remember one time, I don't know if it was Karen or Racquel, once said, "They're calling me names," or "They're calling me chocolate." And I said, "Well, tell them it's your favorite flavor." I know that's what people would say, "Well, think of the kids, you know, it's gonna be hard on them," but I figured if it hadn't been one thing it was going to be another thing—there's always a challenge.

Q What advice might you give to interracial couples or others who are in the same situation as you?

a I don't see why we care about color or religion and all that. I would just make sure that the person is decent and honest. In regard to raising children, I would encourage you not to let people outside of the family get involved in raising your kids because in my experience they interfere and can really mess things up. Trust yourself.

trust yourself

CHAPTER 2
Can I See Your ID?

"What pretty hair! Such lovely color! All mixed people are so beautiful! You people are so sexy and exotic."

This attention may seem flattering at first, but once you have heard it again and again, it starts to get frustrating. While part of our ID is based on appearance, there is much more than meets the eye. Our identity is much more complicated. It is beyond being judged by how we look and includes the same issues as everyone else's—issues such as how we feel about our looks, accepting ourselves, fitting in, feeling sexualized, and trying to figure out who to date. If this isn't enough, we are straddling two or more racial worlds, which can sometimes be very confusing and frustrating but also incredible and amazing. In this chapter, you will learn about the experiences of diverse young women and men that speak directly to issues around dating, stereotypes, socializing, and appearance.

i•den•ti•ty – noun
– the individual characteristics by which a person or thing is recognized

NO ID

Yvonne Sanchez-Tieu

Roaming down the city streets

As empty feelings lead me east.

Turn the corner to my right,

Those streetlights so far in sight,

Glowing, flashing, almost inviting,

Walking down memory lane contemplating,

Who would understand all sides of me?

City lights dimmed, instantly it gets colder, farther so it seems.

Shoulda took the left turn, but how would things have changed?

I've been there before,

Thought it was my friend.

When I got near it read:

Dead end.

So where do I belong?

I guess I'll never know,

As for now I'll be here on these city streets,

Searching for better days,

Lost, empty, and cold,

Yearning for doors to open,

'Cause I've lost my way home.

NOT SO TRADITIONAL

Karuna Sagara

I guess growing up I always expected there to be a bit more Japanese tradition in my family, like all the cool stuff I saw in movies or the things that people *expected* me to know about. Like maybe my family should get together to drink tea on bamboo mats while all the women wear kimonos and the men practice the art of karate.

Okay, I was never that dumb, but I'm not an expert just because of my ancestry. People say things like, "Japanese culture is so rich. Japanese people are so disciplined. The Japanese language is so interesting." Then I say something like, "Really? Can you teach me about it? 'Cause I don't know shit!"

ha·pa – adjective, noun – from Hawaiian ("half") – *slang*; of mixed racial heritage with partial roots in Asian and/or Pacific Islander ancestry – a person of such ancestry – originally a derogatory term, it has since been widely adopted by many multiracial individuals of Asian or Pacific Islander descent, and even by some multiracial non-Asians, as a positive term with which to self-identify

All I know is that I am a *hapa*, which means half-Japanese. My mother's generation is called *Sansei*, which means the third generation of immigrants born in Canada to parents born in Canada, and although she is full-Japanese, she herself doesn't know much about being Japanese.

In all honesty, while I may look the part, it

doesn't really feel right for me to call myself Japanese. It's just as strange for me to say that I am part German, Swedish, Norwegian, Irish, and Scottish, yet this ancestry is just as much a part of me as is my Japanese half. Although I admit there were times when I wished that I was just a little more in touch with my European and Japanese roots, I accept myself as the culturally North American, half-Japanese-looking woman that I am.

B1ack & White

Andrew Ernest Brankley

Hi, I'm white Andrew.

And I'm black Andrew.

We decided, seeing as we both represent part of Andrew, that we should get to know each other better, maybe see where one ends and the other begins.

It was his idea.

Now, now, I think it's important that everyone understands the duality that exists in those of mixed-race background.

Sure.

Cultures differ in whole areas of things, from geography to music, art, dance, language, tradition, religion ... In fact, in any way two people can be different and two people can be similar, we can plausibly assert a culture. There is deaf culture, dwarf culture ... I mean, the list is endless.

True.

What about music? Andrew likes AC/DC, Led Zeppelin, Bob Dylan, Oasis ... Those are fairly white bands, so let's say that's my domain.

So, what—when Andrew likes Jay-Z or DMX, that's my territory?

Yup, that's the spirit!

Okay, well ... let's delve deeper then. I mean without taking a course and studying culture and trying to understand where I am and where you are. Let's just go on intuition. I am white; people seem to envy me or resent me—usually both. I am blamed for a lot of things, because certain white people have done bad things throughout history and for that reason people assume I'm just as bad. I am Andrew when he feels uncomfortable with people of color. I am the butt of jokes when Andrew isn't good at basketball. I am—

Shut up.

Excuse me?

Can you hear yourself go? You are talking like I wasn't there for all those things.

Well, of course you were "there," but I'm just saying those things were more my doing than yours.

Why? Are you saying that every black person is a good basketball player?

Well, no ...

Or that I can't like Led Zeppelin? We both like Jimi Hendrix.

29

No, no, no, you're getting me all wrong.

No, you're getting Andrew all wrong.

I am you; you are me. Everything we do, we do together. When we were born there was one baby; we have one set of genetic code. We don't activate different parts of our brain or souls when we do different things. The hate that people show toward each other, the evil they do isn't   reducible to geography. It's never that simple. This stupid duality is confusing them. Understanding who your parents are is great. Engage in diversity. Coexist with difference. But in the most important ways that make Andrew special, we did it together.

Andrew: True.

INTERRACIAL: OJIBWA, SENECA (MOHAWK), AND MÉTIS

Montana Baerg

In Western society, there are many stereotypes and misconceptions of what Native people's appearances should be. Many people believe that Native women all have darker skin and long black hair, and live in teepees on a reserve, which is not true at all.

One summer, I had the opportunity to work for a Native organization. During that time, I got an urge to dye my hair. I told one of my co-workers that I wanted to dye my hair red and blond. As soon as I told her, she cautioned me to ask my boss before I did anything. So before I went home for the day, I pulled my boss aside and asked her if it would be all right if I dyed my hair those colors. She turned to

Métis – noun – French – a distinct Aboriginal group in Canada – those who can trace their parentage to mixed Aboriginal and European (especially French) descent, and also those who are adopted into this tradition

me with a very **surprised** look on her face and said, "Of course you can—it's your hair. Why wouldn't you be able to dye your hair?"

I explained I thought that maybe everyone who works for a Native organization has to have a certain look. I told her that I didn't look Native to begin with; the only Native thing about me was my long, dark hair, and if I covered it up with red and blond, I wouldn't look Native at all. My boss then told me, "What you look like doesn't determine who you are. If you have **purple** or **red** hair, it doesn't make you any less Native."

WHAT IS YOUR CRAZY FASCINATION?

Janine Berridge

I walk in ...
You stare ...
You smile ...
There's fear in your eyes ...

I look around, wondering why
you would be scared ...
Yes, my hair is curly ... it's not straight ... get over
it ... you went to hair school, didn't you?

Deal with my hair ...
Don't treat
me rudely ...
It's not my fault you aren't
qualified ...
You sit me down in your chair ... play with my hair ... and
say ...
"So what are we doing today?" with a look of prayer in
your eyes for help
I tell you I want a wash, cut, and style ...
"Your hair is so curly, kinky in some parts, smooth in other
areas ... interesting!"
You wash my hair, and your eyes say it all ... I know the
question is coming ...

"What is your background?"
I tell you West Indian Canadian ... that's not good enough
... you want to know specifics ...

I tell you I have black, white,
Spanish, and Indian ...
All of a sudden, you become an expert on
ethnicity and racial characteristics ...
Telling me I have the "body of a black woman,
Latin hair, mixed skin complexion ... Are
you sure you have white in you? I don't see any!"
What the hell is going on? Am I hearing right?
Is this white woman actually telling me this?
I came for a haircut, and instead I get a race examination
What is your crazy
fascination?
If only you could hear
yourself

Hear
your stupidity

As you cut my hair,
I begin to feel uneasy yet again, and feel that another
    dumb comment is about to erupt
I feel another moment that I'll be forced to keep my
    mouth shut
As you ask me how I want my hair styled ... you tell me ...
"You're going to leave it curly, right?"
I know you just don't want to blow-dry my hair ...

It's just such a struggle to go in to the hairdresser
It's just such a struggle to have a pleasant experience
It's just too much pressure ...
Getting my hair done just causes so much inner anxiety
I could go on forever about living and getting my hair done in this confused society.

HAIR, OH, GLORIOUS HAIR

Elizabeth Jennifer Hollo

When I was young my hair grew very long and thick. My father is Hungarian, and in his country the girls' hair grows long. My mother originated from Grenada and when she was young she had really thick hair. It's always been curly, but not those thin curls, the BIG ones that wow people. I've had people come up to me telling me how they wish they had my hair and how beautiful it is and how they could do so much with it. Every morning at the breakfast table, my mom combed out the knots and braided it, and I despised it! All I wanted to do was wear my hair long, no braids, just let it flow. I guess I thought if I did that it would be just like the hair of the white girls in my school who had long luscious hair, soft to touch, shiny, beautiful.

One morning my mother left the room to go look for something and I knew the bus was coming, so I ran as fast as I could out the door and jumped on the bus! My eyes were beaming, my heart was pumping, and then someone said, "Jennifer, what's wrong with your hair?"

I turned my head to the side. "Nothing!" I said, smiling.

I got to school, and all my friends came up to me. "You finally let your hair down!"

I was grinning more than they'd ever seen. "I'm so happy, but it's kinda getting everywhere now." I was pushing it out of my eyes.

"It looks like a black lion's mane," one of the girls said. "Pull it back!" one of them shouted. And so they took charge, pulling it back and putting it up. It definitely wasn't an easy task for them. I never let my hair down for the rest of my time in elementary school.

In middle school I started doing it on my own and buns became the easiest thing for me to do. Then I discovered straightening.

Finally! I saw it: WHITE GIRLS' HAIR! I wanted it; I needed it! But I was forbidden to have it. My mom always told me another thing, "God gave you what you have, don't try to change it!" (I don't know what page of the Bible that came from.) But one day she had a change of heart. "Let me do it," she said while I was struggling with the curling iron. And so it happened: pressed and curled hair. I loved it; I looked like Little Bo-Peep. I was adorable, and the amount of compliments I got that day made me feel like a movie star.

When I got into high school I started straightening it all the time. I didn't have my own straightening iron, so I tried everything from using the curling iron to the regular irons that you iron your clothes with. I'd always wanted my dad's hair because it was straight, easy, and beautiful.

But then I thought about it one day. "Why am I straightening my hair? What is this accomplishing?" So I put the iron down, wet my hair, and put it up. When I looked in the mirror I saw beauty; I saw voluptuous curls that I couldn't get anywhere else. They make me unique; they show both sides of where I come from. They are who I am. My curls are beautiful, and whoever wants to say different, SCREW YOU, because I love 'em! My big head of curly hair is beautiful.

When I looked in the mirror I saw beauty

BLACK BUT NOT SO BEAUTIFUL

Kalale Dalton

I was in seventh grade. I was tender and still impressionable and I was in love, or so I thought. Jacob (not his real name) was of Asian persuasion: cute, smart, and we had been going to the same school since second grade. So after little smiles and stupid fits of giggles finally I worked up the courage to ask our mutual friend to see if he was interested.

So the next day (which, to me, felt like 250 years later), our friend calls me about the hot topic. When I asked him what Jacob said, he started beating around the bush, so I said, "Honestly, just tell me, because even if it's rejection, I can handle it" (which was a complete lie, because I am a big baby and was terrified). Finally, I pried out of him what Jacob had said. He'd said, "I dunno, like, I just think that mixing races would be kind of weird."

"WHATTT!" I screamed. "Are you kidding me?" Was I getting punked? No, no, nope, he did *not* say that. I was livid, and it was speechless anger. I'd never thought that I would ever hear anyone say something like that. My being mixed (black and white) means my whole creation was the result of the coming together of two different races. So I cried. I didn't know what else to do … so I cried. And now as I'm writing, I'm not mad. Now it's kinda funny 'cause he's really ugly, and I can't believe that I ever liked him, but it hurt. I cannot lie, it really hurt.

CHAMELEON lalo lorza

Looking back at all the old pictures I have of my childhood, I'm the only kid who stands out as being different. When I got older and went to high school, all of the people I hung out with were Latin American, and among that group I was always one of the lighter-skinned people. When I'd go back to the hood and chill with my white and black friends, they always referred to me as the "ese," "vato," or Latino guy of the crew. So basically, my white friends didn't acknowledge my white side, my Latino friends made jokes about me   being half-white, and my black friends talked badly about white people, not realizing that my mother is white.

At one point in my life, trying to understand who I was became very conflicting. I didn't know what race I was, what box I belonged in, or if I was being true to myself or not. At times I felt isolated, like there was no one else in the world like me.

My racial identity is a combination of three races: Caucasian, African, and Native American. I have accepted a part of each race; therefore, I don't classify myself as one in particular. I was raised speaking Spanish and English, so I identify as a Latino, but that is not my race. I prefer saying "I'm not white; I'm not black; I'm not red; I'm mixed bred." During the winter, I'm light; during the summer, I'm dark. I'm a man of many cultures and colors, so call me a chameleon.

For anyone out there who's confused about his or her identity, my advice is that you never choose sides; you'll be at peace with yourself only when you acknowledge your roots and become appreciative of who you are. By being mixed, you serve as a reinforced bridge between two or more cultures.

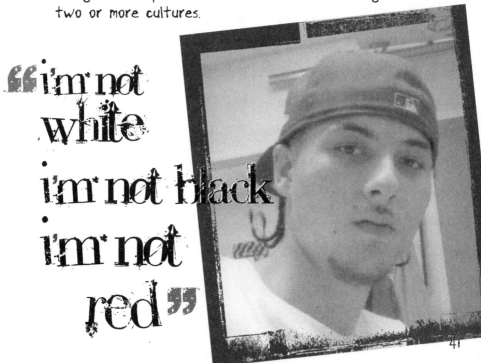

"i'm not white
· i'm not black
· i'm not red "

MIXED DRANKS ON ME

Mia-Skye Sagara

I wanted to fit in, but
you wouldn't let me ... they said, "Naw, she's a
half-breed."
Funny, 'cause you hadn't figured it out, thought i was
Latina,
Mexicana,
Indian ... mixed from indigen, like
just Native to the way you assume.
Leave no room for exceptions, the rules are
deceptive ... thought i had it made the way you praised me.
You liked my long, dark hair, skin touched by
Sunday afternoons in the sun with
my granddaddy ... and i remember
staring into his secret story eyes, wishing i could be
more like him ... you know, whole, full,
perfection ...
Not cut into pieces for quilted depictions of who i was,
unwanted, abused, tricked,
confused ... my pieces are clues.
Follow my footsteps to nowhere, you
couldn't understand even if you tried.
I mean, if i can't explain it any better, and momma's resolve

was always so vague,
then what did you expect to find amongst the
listless days? Oh how you stayed
tryna figure me out.
No room to carve a title,
so i slipped under doors, past
radars that almost had me pegged a coupla times ... too bad
they had it all wrong, but still
he thought i was ... fine.
"She must be mixed," he breathed in heavy, slow gaze,
exoticized me ...
Fantasy for hire, your desires like
ethnic dreams ... to your surprise, that twang i just can't
    shake
threw you off guard like ... what ...
too hood?
Now, this is where some get to cuttin',
into the ribs jokes fly ...
i catch some on a rebound, where
glimpses of my spirit deny and defy your
logic on why i shoulda been more like
someone else you knew who looked just like me.
And oooh! How i love the references, past
present, picture this: some ignorant dude
tryna tell me who I ... Is this dude for real?
Cut the bullshit,
I'm already scarred, been scared too ...
Been up under some shadows heavier than
anything you knew ... i know it sounds
something dramatic, the way i stress the heartbreak, and

confusion magnified by lies,
that touch of vinegar from sour words
you let escape, a few times ...
but picture me on the edge of the ledge of
these boxes i been straddling, i
just couldn't decide ... so tell me,
which one do i jump ... out of?
And all of this over some drinks on a Friday night? Damn,
all i was tryna do was
find my groove, no politics or meaningful depictions of life,
just trying to
work it out ...

He said, "So baby, can you dance?"
Man, here we go ...

NOT JUST SEXY

Text: Karuna Sagara

Poems: Karuna Sagara and Yvonne Sanchez-Tieu

You sexy creature.
Asian doll.
You exotic animal.
You erotic thing, you.
Did you just swim up . . .
from the ocean or the sea?
Who made you?

Now that I look back at my life, I can see how I have contributed to my own sexualization. At a young age I was far more developed than the other girls in my grade and I quickly became aware of the attention that I received. As a young girl going through puberty, I was desperately seeking to find a comfortable sense of self that connected me to others and made me feel special. It's not that I wanted

exot·ic – adjective – originating in or existing in a foreign or distant place – introduced from abroad, but not fully naturalized or acclimatized – attractively or remarkably strange or unusual; bizarre

45

to be sexualized, but my physical form gained me popularity among boys and other developed, popular girls. If I couldn't be the "smart girl" or the "sporty girl," at least I could be the "popular, sexy girl." Of course this role only led me to become labeled as "easy" or "slutty," which of course was a huge offense to me.

Then, as I moved into high school, this identity that I had co-created was only strengthened as I looked so much older than my age and received attention from older males. What teenage girl doesn't want to feel beautiful and have guys notice her? But I began to realize that it was not just my curvaceous figure that was getting me all of this desired attention; I looked different from all the other girls around me. I was ...

Unique, exotic, mysterious,
    Porcelain doll, beautiful creature,
So thick and busty for an Asian girl,
    Definitely more interesting than all of
    the white girls,
        ssssssexy

So then I really, truly was a sexy woman (and I knew it).
"Hey, sexy; you're so sexy; look at your sexy eyes; look at
your sexy hips; let me taste those sexy lips, sexy woman!"
This was the woman I became, the woman I thought I was,
and the woman who I thought I had to be. It was so much of
my identity.

So here I am, years later, and I am still the sexy
woman I've always been. Yes, I am!
But I am more than that. I have
defined myself in many ways, but my
true self is not constricted
by a label. No, that is my
ego wanting to be named,
something, anything ... My
true self is the life
within me.

interview with Tomás sebastian

WHITE BUT BORING

Karen Arthurton

Tomás is a twenty-one-year-old cook who is currently in culinary school at George Brown College. He is half-Chilean and half–Irish Canadian. Karen sat down with Tomás to talk about the concept of "passing." Here is his story.

Q Are there situations when you just pretend that you are the "white dude"?

a Yes, there are times that I totally capitalize on that, especially because there are people who just don't want to know, or some people are so ignorant that they don't even try to say my name or understand why my name is "Tomás" and not "Thomas." It really depends on the situation. Like, in the airport it is just easier to slide through. For example, my brother, who looks like a white guy—he wears glasses and has a beard—brought well over the limit of stuff back from his trip, but he didn't get stopped.

I grew up in a small town. There were a handful of black

> pass·ing – verb – a person classified as a member of one racial group attempting to be perceived or accepted as a member of a different racial group – used especially in the United States during times of slavery or racial segregation to describe a mixed-race person or light-skinned black person whose appearance allowed him or her to move through the world as white

or brown kids that were in my high school. It was just easier to run with the white crowd because it was accepted, it was the norm, something that nobody really questioned or really thought about. Any girlfriend that I had in high school was white but boring. Being the white dude makes it easier to move in the world. Just like the whole popularity thing: people want to be popular in high school; they don't look into culture that much because they focus more on their schoolwork and the social aspects—boyfriends, girlfriends, whatever. In those situations, it is just much easier to be white.

I know I can play the "white card."

Q When people say that you are denying part of who you are, how do you respond to that?

a I first respond by saying that that is not true, it's bullshit, but at the same time it is totally true. I have made peace with that and put it aside and know that I can play the "white card." But as I start to mature, I'm thinking more about my career and my background. To me, sure, you can pass at whatever stage you are at in your life, but in the grand scheme of things high school is four years and the learning that occurs then is not very much (in terms of race or ethnicity). I would agree, though, that I did pass, but now I would laugh in your face if you said that, because I have grown … but I would still do it at the airport. [Laughter.]

Q Do you think other people who pass feel guilt about it?

a I don't think that people feel guilty, because they have done it so much in their lives, or they don't care anymore, or it's just buried in their unconscious. They may be in denial, and it wouldn't even register with them. That's the sad part.

Q What advice would you give to another young person who is "passing" through the world?

a Know that in your soul you are a good person. Be true to yourself. Sometimes you have to hop outside of yourself and connect with your racial backgrounds. Listening to stories from my dad, I am already starting to feel more connected to my Latin history. That is friggin' awesome; that is something that I want to be around. If people can connect to their racial backgrounds on an emotional level, I think it would make them feel so much more comfortable with themselves and being in the real world. Knowing your cultural background is definitely better.

be true to yourself

Excerpt from

itty bitty
A One-Woman Play

Natasha Adiyana Morris

my father has always been into black women
no lighter than heated caramel
but he knows the blacker the berry
flavor his mother had to acquire

early on my father left, she didn't chase
early on he let another man take his place
relieved from responsibility
relieved of respect

my dad is black
my parents raised me proud
equal among my six siblings
it's only ancestral pigment I lack

wrapped in bleeding colors
researched in my cultural herstory
I heal the gazes of illegitimacy
as if my conception was a sin

for I can't undo my yellow complexion
I can't uproot my semi-straight locks
I can't help but be prideful of my heredity
so I don't tolerate that half-breed
pedigree
shit

don't compare me with other "mixed-chicks"
who adopt colonialist tactics
I am conscious of my unfortunate privilege
and feel the unfortunate backlash because of it

resentment is dangerous when fostered in your
own community
I identify as a woman of African descent
check the black box when it's presented
and accept the bastard child identity

they say:
girl you so pritty, pritty, pritty
have it so easy, easy, easy
native?
indian?
brazilian?
puerto rican?

asian?
oh?
canadian
yes.
borderless

pale-skinned people never ask my origin
black
even though my skin is lighter than some of
their own
black
even after the double take
black
but not the regular kind
acceptable

I don't like the false attention
for my light complexion
for those who worship it
are blinded by its corruption
of unearthed weeds
of self-hate and inferiority
to strangle our children's innocence
is passing on wisdom is your priority

Q: why would you want to dread your hair?
A: to lock in your beauty
Q: why would you cut off your locks?
A: to shed the weight of expectations
Q: why do you treat me as your equal?
A: because you are my family, my roots

mi seh, dem weh no have i'
want i'
but dem who have i'
nuh want i'

"I wish I was a little bit lighter,"
said the king, who gave up his throne
"I want my baby to have nice hair,"
said the queen, turned servant
"I want to be like you,"
said their daughter

I don't consider myself mixed-race
but of misplaced biography
I cannot uproot my grandmother's stories
not because she passed, but she's too busy
to pass on herstory
forgetting her past unlocks my future's mystery

I can point out the continent
but not the countries within it
not the endless languages
culture, flavors and spirituality
it's what I'm missing fundamentally
where is home?

but there was a time I was comfortable
head to toe
fearless, round and oblivious
a time where short attention spans had
no room for idleness
and all the time to be curious
a time where I didn't feel the cold
because I couldn't pass up the snow
and picking up adult speech to be witty
and I will never forget childhood adventure
of breathing out color and looking up because
i was itty bitty

CHAPTER 3
My World Around Me

"Where are you from? No, no, where are you really from? Where are your parents from? How come you chill with those people?"

Who we hang out with, where we come from, or who we call family/community is often questioned, but, for better or worse, who we connect with is part of how we make sense of the world. Sometimes, our connections are with family—mom and dad, mom and mom, auntie, or granny. Sometimes we are adopted, and sometimes our friends influence us. Regardless of who we call family or community, we are all looking for places to belong. We all make sense of the world around us in different ways, and community can mean different things to different people. The people who surround and love you may support you, but sometimes they may also judge or hurt you. The world around us, chosen or not, plays a large role in who we are. This chapter speaks about our connection to family and friends, our upbringing, and our communities.

world – noun – a sphere of human activity or interest – a class or group of people with common characteristics or pursuits – the Earth, including all of its inhabitants and the things upon it

Token People, Token Friends

Andrew Ernest Brankley

As people of mixed race, we walk with feet in many different cultural worlds. Often many of them collide because of the prejudices and stereotyping that individuals assign not only to other cultures but also to their own. From a young age, children join social groups in a variety of different environments. As they mature, their roles within those groups become clear: "That's the funny guy, that's the sports star, that's the pretty girl, that's the smart guy … that's the token black guy." Some people think they are better people by including someone who's different and that they are being kind. In a way they are. I'm not arguing that trying to include people who are different is wrong, but when you limit their role to being your "token race friend," it is.

Coming from a mixed-race background makes it easier for groups to include you, and easier to stereotype you. Because mixed-race individuals share cultures with those of a single race they are more likely to associate with them. However, when their new friends find out they have a little race *x* inside them, they feel good: "Hey, now I have a black friend!" This leads to increased racial humor and stereotyping. I've had friends make racist jokes around me, saying, "Hey, it's okay, right, Andrew?" The pressure this puts on people of mixed race to go along with prejudice is tremendous. They have to choose among being included in the group, risking social anxiety by being excluded, or standing up for themselves.

I have no easy answers. You shouldn't have to choose insult or loneliness. Either choice leaves you hurt. Stick up for yourself, but don't isolate yourself either. Remember that people are never as bad as they seem to be. There are situations where people aren't trying to be racist; they actually are, in their own way, reaching out. If you have the courage, meet them "half" way.

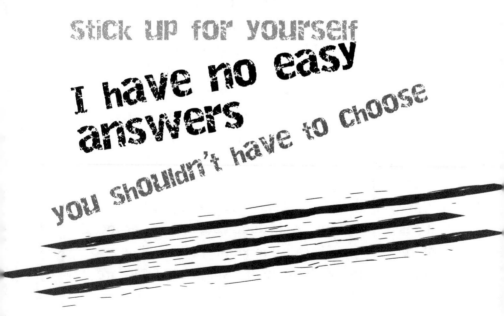

Stick up for yourself

I have no easy answers

you shouldn't have to choose

Navigating Through Culture: Finding My Way Home

Yvonne Sanchez-Tieu

Coming from a place where I struggled for many, many years about who I am and where I fit in, looking in the mirror and seeing two different people, can be very weird. It was from a lack of acceptance of my being mixed that led me to adapting to whatever cultures would accept me.

At first, this was the African Canadian culture. Being very young and not fitting in with those of my kind, I was hanging out with all the mixed and black kids. They were accepting and did not judge me based on color. I started making better friends that were not judgmental, prejudiced, or discriminating and really building relationships with the mixed and black kids. I even started to like black guys. I learned about their culture while searching for a place to belong, finding that place, and being engulfed in it. I was very comfortable at the time; some would argue that I'd adopted their culture and thought I was one of them. It didn't matter to me. For once I felt relevant, accepted, and that I belonged. It was a good feeling. Screw what anybody else says, right?

So after years of hanging out with mostly black friends and dating mostly black guys, I started to feel that something wasn't right. How was I, a visibly mixed person of Latino and Asian descent, without relations of any sort with my own people? A part of me wanted to explore this question. And so I began to look into myself. I took myself away from what I knew and wanted to know about the unknown. I mean, having been exposed to and accepted by black people and their culture was a great experience. I learned a great amount from that; however, I couldn't live the rest of my life knowing that I was visibly different from all my friends and that I couldn't relate to my roots.

Anyway, I started just being me, not really caring anymore about anything or anyone. I became a lot more open-minded as I journeyed through the world with conflicting views, because I knew I had to be to become enlightened.

My journey goes on as I try to figure myself out in this world, and as time goes on, I become more real and true to myself. I now identify myself as a mixed-race person, proud of my culture, and still learning and growing every day, eager to become more enlightened of the cultures that make me: Latina and Southeast Asian.

ONE THING LEADS TO ANOTHER

Justin Robinson

Fitting in with friends can be crucial. I grew up in one hood, but I went to school in another. The school I went to happened to have a lot of Spanish kids, and, well, let's just say it was a multicultural school. Now ever since elementary, there has been a feud between black and Spanish kids in that neighborhood.

My two best friends were Isaiah and Matthew, one black and the other Spanish, and I just happen to be half-Latino and half-black. Isaiah was an interesting kid. He loved basketball and loved girls, but was the younger brother of the baddest kid in school, who is now notorious in that hood. Matthew was a funny Spanish kid. No matter what, he would make everyone break out in tears from laughing; now he's Isaiah's biggest beef.

Isaiah and Matthew hated each other; they were actually part of that black vs. Spanish feud. As we entered high school, things became different. Girls were better-looking, and there were a hundred times more kids than there were in elementary school. But what stood out were the crews. There was a crew named S.V., aka Street Villains, and one named M.M., Most Matos, or something along those lines. Within a month I heard Isaiah was rollin' with S.V. and Matthew was already hurtin' people because he was a part of M.M.

I was caught dead center of it all. They both tried to lure me in. "I" would be like, "You're black, Dawgy, let's roll." Matt would be like, "Come on, J. Bone, I'm your best friend." See, to be in either crew you had to be black or Spanish. I was only in grade nine and I had one of the hardest decisions of my life to make. So I just went nuts on everyone. I was bullying kids, I was robbing people, I got tattoos, and I called myself "Job." I got kicked out of school for two months.

My mom told me she had found another school that was close to our home. When I got there I instantly noticed everyone was hanging with their own ethnicity. I didn't know anyone. I would skip school and just hang out by myself every day. I'm not saying I was a lonely person; I just didn't trust anyone. So then again, because I didn't fit in with anyone, I became Job. I started robbing people again. I started hurtin' people. Then I was arrested. I was in and out of jail. I didn't care about anything. I bought cars, big TVs, PS3s, brand-new cell phones. I became the talk of the town; now everyone loved me, but I hated it.

While on house arrest for a string of robberies, the judge gave me the weirdest deal: if I were to prove myself in the community, then I would get a light sentence.

62

For months, I worked my ass off. I was known in many different community centers. I was in hoods I would have never ever gone to before, just to mentor little kids. I was becoming Justin again. Because I had been Job before and everyone knew me as that guy who does whatever he wants, I was embarrassed. I didn't wanna be him anymore. From May 2009, I told everyone they ain't gonna see me anymore. I was going on the low. It was a very difficult time. I was lost. I honestly didn't know who I was.

I got off house arrest November 6, 2009, but I was still on the low. In December when I met Karen and Karuna, who were putting this book together, I was blown away 'cause I had no clue that people actually cared about being mixed. When I look back and think of the path I've taken, you could say this was meant to be. If there hadn't been a problem at my elementary and high schools, I wouldn't have become Job, and I wouldn't have gone to jail, and I wouldn't have met Nakisha, who gave me Karen's number, and to be honest if it wasn't for this project I have no clue where I would be. This is a lifesaver, and I'm very thankful for every bit of it.

A Different World

Jelissa Pamplona

The elementary school I went to was in a Portuguese neighborhood, so the whole school was made up of Portuguese students and teachers, with the exception of about four black people and myself. I'm mixed black, Nova Scotian, and Portuguese. I was probably the only mixed child in the school. Even though I was half-Portuguese and half-black, everyone at school just considered me black. I guess it was because of my features and my hair, but it really bothered me because I was equally both. I hated the fact that I was always put into one category. My friends didn't know it bothered me that much, though. I never showed it to them, only to my family. Sometimes I would go home and cry about it, that's how much it bothered me. All my friends and boyfriends were white. When I was dating a boy from school I was always conscious of how people would look at us or what people would think.

no categories—just mixed

64

When I would go over to my aunt's house (on my Scotian side) all my cousins would bother me about the way I was dressed and the way I talked. They always called me "whitewash." So with my cousins, I felt like I had to ACT a certain way, and at school I felt like I had to BE a certain way.

When I got to high school, it was a completely different atmosphere. There were Portuguese, Spanish, Filipino, and a lot of black people, something I was definitely not used to—a mix of different kinds of people. I became good friends with a whole bunch of black people, a group I was barely seen hanging out with back in elementary school. I was no longer categorized as just "white" or "black." For the first time I was just me, just mixed. I didn't have to act or be a certain race to impress anybody anymore. My cousins stopped with all their comments, and I even dated a couple of black guys. So for me, going from elementary school to high school was like walking into a different world, no categories—just mixed.

Chocolate or Milk

WHAT'S YOUR FAVORITE FLAVOR?

"Angelina Jones"

Since I was young I've had a wide variety of friends. When I became interested in guys, the types of smile never mattered, the language never mattered, and the race never mattered. I remember when I was in grade two and an Indian boy told me he liked me … I mean … he REALLY liked me! All I could do was laugh, until middle school hit and I found out who I really was: The "thick-boned, green-eyed, light-skinned with booty" girl. That was my title for many years, whether it was walking down the street with my mom and dad or even with my friends. Gradually over time I adopted a group of African American friends who I was with every day and who managed to change my persona and views about everything.

With my new group of friends everything around me started to change—the way I dressed, acted, and even who I was interested in. I started to be attracted only to African American males, specifically those with brown skin, short-trimmed or long, well-maintained hair, with a nice smile or nice eyes. My attraction to brown guys really was about the tone: they were in the middle, not dark-skinned or light-skinned. I'm still more attracted to brown-skinned men, like the companion I am with now.

Being biracial has become oh-so popular and the new trend. I feel more like an object instead of a human being when people refer to me as "that mixed girl." This is painful enough without thinking about restricting my choices of attraction. You can't help being attracted to a certain type, or help where you come from, but it makes you who you are. Being thick and having an attraction to African Canadian men, I never attracted the typical white boy.

My circle of white male friends explained to me that the majority of them didn't really like black girls. Knowing this and not being such a risk taker, I've always stuck to brown-skinned guys and personally, because I'm such a lighter shade of light skin, I feel like dating someone with my complexion would make me and my companion look more like brother and sister. Most people think that all light skins are cousins, brothers, sisters, or some sort of family member. I'm happy with my color and my choice of those I'm attracted to.

From all this I can only say, follow your heart and not the color of someone's skin because everybody has amazing characteristics. I learned this from both my white and black sides of family who came together to have, raise, and love me.

The Blind Side

Lynnea Jones

I've grown up with Natives and consider myself full

Yet there's a whole half I don't even know

No one knows who he is or where he's from

Except for my dearest mom

She raised me since birth, but now that I'm older

There's this one wish I've had for so many years
   with no questions answered

I've grown quite frustrated and my brain is clustered

Filled with thoughts of who he could be

Wondering if he's ever known about me

There's a piece of me missing that hasn't been found

And with every new day that passes me by

I grow more and more worried and understand why

The hourglass is turned and I don't mind dying

Just I'd rather die knowing who I am than not
   knowing at all

So when I shut my eyes and relax my mind

I'm proud that I'm Ojibwa

Family Picture

Janine Berridge

I am feeling very overwhelmed because I have tried to forget how screwed up everyone is. I don't understand why you hate everyone's race when inside you are everything you hate.

You are black, you are Indian, but somehow you deny that part of you and hate everything about anyone that reminds you of that part of you. You love your Portuguese side, and anything in you that is remotely white and full of privilege. Any time I connect with anything that strays from whiteness, all hell breaks loose. I have no idea how you married my father, since he has no problem speaking out against your craziness and your family's similar delusions.

My family is filled with identity confusions. I can see them quite clearly and find myself among the circus. The joke that you all seek to live within is a laugh, not only

to me but also to all the "real" white folk. Because your acting "white" and associating with privilege in their eyes is nothing but a joke. The ones you are trying to associate with—because apparently whiteness brings rightness—see you as just another colored person and will never accept you as their own.

I think it's time you all leave that old small-island mentality where you sat once with queens and kings alone. You need to realize that here, if we are not white, we are all in a fight. When I look at my family portrait, I see confusion, I see different races, I see different hair, I see different accents, I see different countries, all struggling to be white, all with colored faces. All struggling to find their places.

**I see different accents
I see different countries**

Assimilation, Assimilation

Karuna Sagara

Each year for almost every major holiday, my family gets together at one of my mom's cousins' houses and has a huge Japanese North American–style dinner. There is always a minimum of about twenty-five family members and at times, when my extended family's extended family shows up, we can get up to forty people. I think that my family is as tight as they are because of the experience of having their whole world stolen from

them and then forced into internment camps together in interior British Columbia during World War II. The only way my grandfather and his siblings' families were able to rebuild their lives after that dark period was to squeeze together in my grandfather's little bungalow and start fresh in Toronto.

Back in those days, discrimination toward Japanese people was far more prevalent. The sure way to show you were not an evil, Pearl Harbor—bombing Jap was to assimilate and throw out your Japanese culture like it was spoiled food. So aside from losing their language and

their customs, it seems like Japanese people made an effort to dilute their Japanese blood with white blood until it disappeared completely. That's why, if you look around at all of the faces at our family gatherings, you'll see that as the generations get younger, they become more and more mixed with white. I am not at all against interracial couples, as I am proud to be the product of one, but when I hear things like "Ninety-five percent of Japanese Americans are in mixed marriages" ... I don't know ... it kind of disappoints me. I think part of it is because I am aware of the fascination with Western culture that Japanese people have, and it's like being with a white person will bring them to the "right" side faster.

I remember a time in my teenage years when I thought to myself, What the hell, if things keep going the way they're going, our Japanese ancestry will disappear completely! I thought it could be my personal mission to make sure that the Japanese bloodline remained in my family. All that I needed to do was to have children with a Japanese man, but when I thought about it, I realized I didn't really know many Japanese people other than my family. Maybe this is the reason for all of the Japanese mixed marriages; Japanese people are so assimilated and dispersed around the country that you can barely find them.

just like us— Twinkies

I did end up dating a half-Japanese, half—French Canadian guy when I was eighteen. We talked about how cool it would be to have kids together because they would be just like us—Twinkies—but we never got to that point. He ended up marrying a white woman. After that, I decided to end my mission and allow myself to love someone not because of their mix, their race, or their ethnicity, but because they were an amazing human being who loved me too.

LOSS Of ONe Half Of Me

Elizabeth Jennifer Hollo

I was a little girl. Not like I feel now, like there's a whole side of me missing, like the structure of my life was nuked. It was nuked the moment I lost my dad. It's really hard to write about my dad, but it's also really important. He is half of me, half of my heritage. I can't ignore him.

My dad was Hungarian. He had many sides to him. There was the kind, gentle, giving, courteous side. Then he had the temper of a bull that is being teased with a waving, red silk cloth. Then he had his happy side where he sung, made up poems in Hungarian off the top of his head, and joked around while laughing as hard as he could, drinking away merrily, not caring about a thing. Then the quiet, deep-thinking sensitive man I saw at times, with the silent love he shared with the people he cared for. He had so much in common with me, although I didn't know till now as I think back—taking the time to remember the person he was, the little things that matter so much more now, and the culture he craved so badly to share with me. I knew he loved me just as much as I loved him, but we never know what we have till it's gone.

When I was little he would teach me how to be independent. We would go to my auntie's house for Christmas, and they would all play Hungarian cards. Even though I didn't speak much Hungarian, he always knew I understood. He would teach me how to speak it; he wanted me to know his heritage. He was so close to me. I know I was his baby, always will be his *cicuska* ("little kitty" in Hungarian), and he'll always be with me.

A year and a half ago, my dad died; a year before that, he got sick.

My mom spent every day by his side, but I couldn't do it. I couldn't see him like that: paralyzed on the right side, brain dead. I couldn't hear his voice, couldn't understand him, and didn't know if he could understand me. Our family just went on with their lives, like we weren't suffering, like it wasn't happening. Christmas came and went, Thanksgiving, Easter, the long, cold, winter months, his birthday and all of ours, Father's Day, Mother's Day; it all passed by as did the memories in my mind.

He ended up at Saint Joseph's [Hospital]. They sucked out the fluids in his stomach as we watched him die for days. They claimed they couldn't do anything for him, and we didn't have any more say in the matter. I would hold his hand, and he would watch as endless tears fell out of my eyes, not having enough strength to wipe them away. Not having the voice to tell him it's going to be okay. I remembered when I would lie

there is a point in life when everything changes

on his stomach and tell him his beer belly was my pillow, and he would laugh and we'd watch television till I'd fall asleep. Now, he had got so bony, so unrecognizable, it was heartbreaking and traumatizing.

There is a point in life where everything changes for better or for worse.

Now, I've never felt so lost. I feel like there's a bullet that's still burning, lodged in my heart. Life fell apart when he got sick, and when he died, even more so. I feel like half of me is gone, and there's no way of getting it back. The half of me that connected with my Hungarian roots is no longer visible, so it feels that part of my heritage, parts of my roots, are gone. The side of me connected with Grenadian roots lives on, but the Hungarian heritage of my dad lives on in memory because he was that important to me.

Sadly, family issues arose from this: it's like an earthquake happened, and now my dad's side of the family and my mom's side are drifting far apart on different sides of the earth. And who's the one stuck on a little raft in the middle of that big ocean? Me. Just drifting, hoping they'll both come back together to save me one day. Losing him in the middle of so many other things going on in my teenage life was the hardest thing I could ever have gone through.

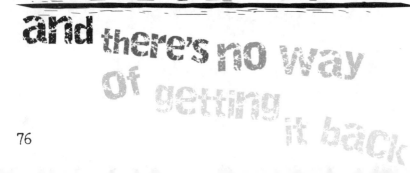

half of me is gone

and there's no way of getting it back

MISMATCH

Kalale Dalton

I am a black person growing up in a white family. To the world, I am not a white person. But if they knew me, my home, my world, my family, it wouldn't be any different than "Jackie Smith's" down the street. But still I don't belong.

For my eighteen years of life, I have lived with my openly artistic, beans-and potato-eating, cottage-going, salt-of-the-earth, back-in-two-shakes-of-a-lamb's-tail white father—in the middle of downtown Toronto. Before I was born in the late eighties, my father, in his funkier days, helped conceive my older sister. My twenty-three-year-old, strong-willed, never-take-no-bullshit, as-beautiful-as, secret-keeping, Barbies-till-dawn, partner-in-crime, light-of-my-life, woman-I-hope-to-become sister, who is white. My stepmom is the crazy, Saks Fifth Avenue-shopping, pour-me-another-glass,

mu·lat·to — noun, adjective — likely from the Spanish and Portuguese word *mulato* ("young mule"; a mule is the hybrid offspring of a horse and a donkey) and connected to Spain's central role in the Atlantic slave trade — person of mixed white and black heritage — although still in wide use and not labeled offensive in most English-language dictionaries, the term is rejected by many because of its etymology — alternative terms are *mixed race* or *biracial*

laugh-like-the-sun, the-best-for-my-girls, Sunday-matinee, stronger-than-she-looks, free-spirited mother of my sister, and she is white. So then where is the handbook on how to be black that everyone assumes I must have read?

To onlookers, my inside and my outside don't match. They say, "Why does that light-skinned, whitewashed, Uncle Tom, mulatto-lookin' black girl talk like that, look like that, love like that?" And what can I say? It is confusing, but this is who I am. I am defined by myself, and I haven't decided yet!

STIR-FRY

Chiloh Turner

Stir-fry some rice. Couple vegetables, a little spice, and we got something nice.

Growing up in a house with five other siblings, our mom, and our dad was totally normal. I mean, who knew anything different? Our dad worked and brought home the cheddar, while our mom maintained the household and looked after the children. I guess you can say we were one big, happy family.

As the years went on and I got older, I began to realize that our mom was our mom, but our dad wasn't really our dad. He was MY dad. At first I was like, WHAT? Is that even possible for siblings to have different parents? I mean, I was confused. Was I black; was I white? Were they black, or were they white? For HEAVEN'S SAKE! I couldn't tell, because the majority of us are light-skinned. It took some ironing out the

wrinkles to put things in perspective and to realize that I wasn't the only "freak" with a different father in our household. As I got older, everything made sense.

chocolate brown sugar caramel

Among me and my siblings, I was the lightest one. Then there's Shanae, who's the darkest one (my chocolate), followed by Shannon, who's in-between (brown sugar). Next up, there's Shaquira and Shaun, who are a little darker than me, and Shatrese (caramel). And last but not least, Sharese, who mimicked my color but she was born with freckles, and I was born glowing like the sun. I guess you can really say ... STIR-FRY!

interview with veronica salvatierra

A YOUNG LATINA MOM TALKS ABOUT RAISING A MIXED CHILD

lalo lopza

Veronica Salvatierra was born in Argentina to parents of Chilean descent. She was raised in Canada. She gave birth to her daughter, who is mixed Argentine-Grenadian, when she was nineteen years old, and raised her as a single mother. Veronica began studying correctional services at college when her daughter was two years old and has been working with youth for the past thirteen years.

Q Do you accept or identify your daughter as black, Latina, or mixed?

a I consider her West Indian and Latina. People always have the idea that when a child is mixed, they become less of both cultures, when actually, at least in my opinion, they're both. If you're going to have children, then you have to learn to accept everything they are.

Q Was there any pressure from your parents to raise your daughter with purely Hispanic traditions?

a Luckily my family has been very supportive of me and the way that I want to raise my daughter and they've always trusted my decisions. I pressured myself to raise her knowing both of her cultures and knowing both sides of her family—simply because she isn't only Latina.

81

Q What did your family think about you having a mixed-race child?

a My mother never said anything negative, at least not to me. My father on the other hand hated the fact that the father was a black man because he was a traditional Latino man and wanted me to be with a traditional Latino man. Straight up, he was racist. Initially, it was hard for him to accept and because we didn't have a relationship it bothered him even more. But once she was born and he got to know the father, they actually became friends and he loves my daughter like any grandfather.

Q Did you experience any challenges from people other than your family?

know BOth cultures

a I found the public, especially in the mid-1990s, to be really judgmental. I would take my daughter out in the stroller, and people would give me dirty looks. It was really upsetting. I had a baby face and people would talk bad about me having a mixed child. I could hear them saying things—things I don't care to repeat. I found that older people were the worst.

Q Was there anything you're glad you had to learn while raising your daughter?

a I learned to cook certain foods, both Latino and West Indian dishes. I had to learn how to take care of her hair and skin, how to share her with both families just like everyone else, bite my tongue instead of talking bad about the other side of the family, and to work together with her father through the differences. I'm glad I raised her this way because she identifies with both of her cultures and is proud of both of them …You have to be inclusive. I learned that it was my responsibility to learn about her other culture—the foods, the sounds—and I learned that it's healthy for [mixed-race children] to identify with all the cultures that are in them because that is the only way that they will be whole.

 Do you have any advice for other parents of mixed-race children?

I'd say keep good communications with both sides of your child's family, and give your child the opportunity to know both cultures. I also recommend that you never say anything negative around your child about their heritage. Give them the opportunity to grow with the richness of the cultures they are.

"the only way that they will be whole"

MY ADVICE TO PARENTS

A MIXED DAUGHTER'S PERSPECTIVE

Mia-Skye Sagara

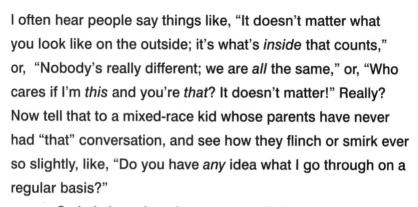

I often hear people say things like, "It doesn't matter what you look like on the outside; it's what's *inside* that counts," or, "Nobody's really different; we are *all* the same," or, "Who cares if I'm *this* and you're *that*? It doesn't matter!" Really? Now tell that to a mixed-race kid whose parents have never had "that" conversation, and see how they flinch or smirk ever so slightly, like, "Do you have *any* idea what I go through on a regular basis?"

So let's keep it real, we are *not* all the same, and you can sugar-coat it if you'd like to, but at the end of the day, each one of us has a unique story to tell and a personal struggle that is all our own. Some of that is based largely on how the world perceives us and how we identify ourselves within the world. Now take two or more of those cultural identities and mix them together, then slap a few labels and stereotypes onto them, dice 'em up and then, just for fun, put them all back together again into whatever *one box* you see *fit* that day based on, say … hair texture, skin tone, eye or nose shape, and lip fullness, *et voilà*! You've got a mixed-race person.

Now this isn't meant to scare any of you expecting parents awaiting a mixed child, or even parents of a mixed child with whom you've never discussed the topic. It's just a precursor of what *may* be to come. And sure, some of us struggle a lot less. Heck, some of us have never had *any* of these issues and are given the language early on to self-identify, *never* experiencing any confusion of cultural identity whatsoever. But here's the catch: you can't ever predict how your child will eventually look, feel, be perceived, or see themselves in life and in the world. So it then becomes *your*

responsibility not only to teach your child about where they come from, and I mean about *all* sides, but also to be sensitive to their questions of identity and race. Not having an open dialogue about race can not only hurt and confuse mixed-race

children but also quite possibly alienate them from society and oftentimes their own families. This is more important than you could imagine, especially for a parent who is *not* mixed and has never experienced being mistaken for another race or ethnicity, or maybe even dealt with racism at *all*.

The problem lies in how parents deal with the responsibility of having a mixed child and whether or not they are prepared for it, or have even thought about that child's future cultural identity. It's interesting how when you are a little kid none of that matters; you're just cute and everyone loves you. It's not until a mixed-race child grows up into a mixed-race adult that the attitudes of family and sometimes even friends often change, as do the relationships, based mostly on the level of people's own comfort with the young adult and his or her changing ethnic identity. Sadly it comes down to a sort of bidding war, one side trying to win the mixed-race person over, claiming he or she is *more* like *them*.

Now that I have my own daughter who is mixed (as I am myself mixed and would have inevitably had a mixed child no matter what), I often wonder how she will be perceived in the world and how she will feel about herself as a mixed-race person ... *or* if she will even care. It will depend on how her own experiences, as well as how others perceive her. I guess the responsibility in raising a mixed child is a never-ending process of staying alert and open to your child's ever-changing self-identity, and exposing them to their own cultural heritages as much as possible through story, literature, film and the arts, community (even if not your own), and family. As with everything, remaining open-minded and honest is essential in trying to understand your mixed child.

Now that I am older and my insecurities of not fitting in have subsided, I am left with a sense of greater peace and, more important, a certain freedom in knowing I am bound by no rules for who I must be, standing proudly on the outskirts with an outside perspective. There will always be those who expect me to be the person they perceive me as, but I no longer feel the need to defend myself or to argue who that may or may not be. Although my journey has been long and often heartbreaking, I feel it has better prepared me for raising my own mixed daughter, giving me the language and compassion one needs for such a unique experience in the world. I pray she will love herself, and that the questions she poses in her mind will be answered, and that she will find an identity to call her own no matter what that is. I pray that she embraces all the parts that make up her beautiful, original mixed self, and above all else, I hope as any parent would, that she is truly happy within her own rainbow body.

a unique experience

beautiful, original mixed self

no rules for who I must be

CHAPTER 4
Above and Beyond Race

What is amazing about being of mixed race? What are the gifts and strengths? Who are you beyond race? When will you be seen for just being you—no race, no age, just you?

Our journey together ends here, but the discovery of who we are in life continues. As we grow and change, race will become less important as we discover that it is only one aspect of our beautiful selves. There will always be challenges; however, the process will take us above and beyond race to a road of self-discovery. This final chapter talks about our gifts, talents, and strengths, and the positive vibes and lessons learned from the experiences that life has given us. It's not just about race. We are human beings and we are freakin' amazing!

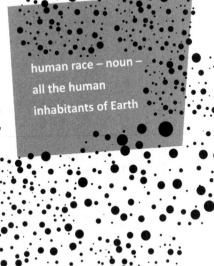

human race – noun – all the human inhabitants of Earth

No Matter How Many Times

Janine Berridge

No matter how many times you ask me,
"What are you?"
No matter how many times I look around the room
And don't see any allies in sight
No matter how many times you say, "You can't be black, or Indian
    or …" and it goes on,
but then you say, "Well, maybe … kinda … I guess you kinda look
    like …"
No matter how many times you tell me, "But your hair is too curly
    to be white … it's so
kinky right there, but you can't be …"
No matter how many times I hear, "You're shit," will I lose my
    bliss … myself
No matter how many times you stare at me like some museum
    artifact
No matter how many times I hear your whispers
No matter how many times you kiss your teeth,
    roll your eyes, despise, will my spirit die
And no matter how I feel your envy of me creep up my
    spine from your hating eye …
I will not give in to your ignorance, your pressure, your
    conformity, misguided
interpretations, and flirtations to fit
    me into your comfortable view of life.

THE WAY I AM

Justin Robinson

I am a mix of dark and darker
I am black and Spanish
Sometimes being both is a great thing,
and I fit in anywhere
But sometimes I feel rejected by both
and am nowhere
I have two cultures, and this is a good thing
Although sometimes I think it would be
easier to be one
I know rituals and languages for two different
worlds
This sometimes tests my knowing who I am
I try to take the best from both these heritages
and learn from the worst
This gives me an opportunity most people
don't have
So I think I will always choose the way I am.

interview with carol camper

PART TWO

Yvonne Sanchez-Tieu

Q You are the editor of *Miscegenation Blues*, an anthology of work by mixed-race women. What inspired you to be part of this book?

a I was inspired by meeting a lot of young people, particularly women in their twenties, as I got more involved in community politics and activism—and a lot of them were of mixed heritage. I had noticed that they seemed to have some trouble with issues of belonging or fitting in. I sensed what I felt was a kind of loneliness and lack of connection to community, and uncertainty, like, "Where do I fit?" The issues of people who are mixed because of the mixed marriage of their parents, rather than mixing that happened centuries ago, are a little bit different. People whose racial mix happened many generations ago may have been able to grow up in communities with

Where do I fit?

people who look like them and have a common experience, and they may not identify as mixed, and they certainly wouldn't feel alienated within their own family group. But when one parent is white and one parent is of color, sometimes there's a lot of alienation that kids from those relationships experience.

I noticed that, and I wanted to help some of those people find their way into feeling okay about their own journey and feeling hope and feeling some kind of connection, and to encourage them to feel really, really great about being exactly who they are.

Q What are some of the gifts, privileges, and positive things about being of mixed race?

a I feel a little subversive sometimes, and I might just be outside of people's expectations sometimes, and I like that. I don't want to be a provocateur, but, yeah, I guess I sort of like part of the not fitting in if it means I'm perhaps less predictable. I guess sometimes as a person who grew up very isolated from any community that looks like me and alienated in a lot of ways, I actually kind of like it that I look like a bunch of different racial groups. So I felt in a way homeless in my soul as a child and so what it means is that suddenly I have all these new homes that I can be a part of. I like the idea of fitting into many cultures; maybe I would even be able to slide in and out of those cultures for fun or for whatever reason. But politically I don't take the stand that I have the best of both worlds when it comes

mis·ce·gen·a·tion – noun – the interbreeding of people of different racial types; especially the interbreeding of whites and non-whites – marriage between people of different races – starting in the early seventeenth century and remaining in force in many U.S. states until 1967, anti-miscegenation laws enforced racial segregation by criminalizing interracial marriage and sometimes also sex between members of different races

to my looks and physicality. I don't like that kind of statement because it implies that there is something wrong with my racial origins, usually the black ones, and that the white part of me has been able to mitigate them and make them less disturbing or more palatable to whoever's looking at me, so I don't like that "best of both worlds" thing. There might be some bad things about being white and what white looks like, but this culture doesn't really spell that out. This culture does spell out what's wrong with looking too black or too Native American.

Q What is your advice to other young mixed-race people facing some of the challenges of being mixed-race in today's society?

a I would say to educate yourself about racism, particularly about the subtly of racism, and I think that everyone, including people of color, has to do some self-interrogation about their own racism. To me, you can't grow up in a racist society without becoming racist, so you know we're not racism-free because we're not white. It's not as simple as that, and some of us have negative feelings toward our "of color" part. We need to investigate that, challenge ourselves, rid ourselves of that. I think we all need to be patient with one another around our differences, and talk. It's important to talk instead of making assumptions, so that's what I would say to young people: read, talk, investigate, have patience, and approach one another from a position of being open and willing to learn and love.

COMPLEX SIMPLICITY

lalo lopza

I'm a mixed man, a complex product of the white plan
To thin out other cultures by the nightstand
So they created this Hispanic with a slight tan
To roam the earth and carry light in his right hand
Got the blood of Chibchas, Africans, and the Norse
The perfect balance of intelligence, wisdom, and force
My ancestors survived genocide, the middle passage
And the Irish famine; I'm what happens when three
worlds collide
I feel like a science experiment
But at the same time, I give thanks for the experience
I'm still viewed as a minority in the eyes of the oppressor
In other words, a being that's lesser
'Cause I'm living in a world run by Europeans
Where the dreams of colored people get crushed; it's
been this way for eons
But I learned to understand this situation I was given
And now I'm really livin'.

BALANCE

Alexandre Nahdee

*It is all about
Finding balance in your own
Life and existence …*

For me, it's about finding balance in your own existence because if you start identifying yourself as being half-Native and half something else, you are splitting your spirit and identity. When you do this, you're not acknowledging that, in actuality, you exist on the Earth as one person and not two. For me, having parents that come from different parts of the world allowed me to realize, despite the differences, that the similarities are stronger. This shows me that people can exist, work, and be happy with one another.

ON A POSITIVE NOTE

Yvonne Sanchez-Tieu

My journey as a mixed-race young woman has taught me a great amount of valuable things. I think mixed people are so special; kind of like the best of both worlds. There is so much beauty in us. We are bright, creative, open-minded, adaptable, diverse, unique, etc. It's just sad to see it get lost in the eyes of ignorant people, because we don't fit into a category and they can't classify us. Does that mean we're any less than, or less of, anybody or anything? No, if anything we're more than, and better than, because we are of multi-race, so in a sense we have a broader sense of mind.

i would not change a thing

It allows us to be more open-minded as we experience things that a nonmixed person would not experience or understand. A lot of us are also multicultural, adapting to various sides of our heritage. We shouldn't have to pick or choose a side; we should embrace the diversity of our people and recognize that we are nothing less or different, and celebrate the fact that we

are all one race and all beautiful. There are
so many wonderful things that come with being a
mixed-race person. Although there are struggles
and challenges we face in society, the learning
experience through the journey and all the
positive things make it worth going through. I
would not change a thing about my background.
I love my heritages; I have accepted
myself as a beautiful, young,
mixed-race woman.

"i have accepted myself"

RAINDROP

Chiloh Turner

Ever since I could remember lightskinn
Was the right skinn ...
I mean beautifull ...
Like something exotic ...
Or something melodic ...
Praised and phased ...
Dazed and amazed ...
But a new train of thought ...
Fluster my vision ...
So I close my eyes and listen ...
Stunned by how much one's words could make
someone feel ...
Filthy half-breed/mule ...
This could turn out to be a duel ...
But I take a deep breath ...
And conserve my cool ...
Because I ...
I'm on a higher pedestal...
I could cut you up ...

Or break you down ...

But that would only make me look like a fool ...

I'm tired, so so tired of all this excess drool...

I'm a MISTAKE!!

FAKE!!

A rip-off of all the races in my make ...

Ever since I could remember lightskinn ...

Was the right skinn ...

I mean beautifull ...

Like something exotic ...

Or something melodic ...

Praised and phased ...

Dazed and amazed ...

It's time for me to open my eyes ...

And realize ...

That all you beak ...

Are bullshit lies ...

But I'm not mad ...

Do you know why? ...

Because I'll leave it in God's hands ...

One day you will see ...

That all of us are ONE ...

INFINITY.

ADVICE FOR PARENTS AND CAREGIVERS

Karen Arthurton

As a mixed-race parent raising a mixed-race child, I have learned a lot from my own experiences and from the mixed-race youth I work with. Parenting has no manual that gives us all the answers for raising our children, but here are a few suggestions that may help when raising a mixed-race person.

- Talk to your kids about race and racism, and how it affects them.
- If you are of mixed race, share your own experiences: the struggles and the gifts.
- Be supportive of how the child identifies. He or she may choose to identify with a racial group you do not identify with, but allow your child to make choices and to grow from his or her experiences.
- Promote the learning of languages, cultures, and history. Help your children understand the many backgrounds that they are from. This may help them later on in life when they are trying to discover who they are.
- Document your own history or the history of your partner (or other parent). There are pieces of our own background that we may need to learn or relearn in order to teach our children.
- Be aware of and know how to manage issues surrounding self-esteem and self-identity, such as physical appearance (specifically hair texture and skin tone), sexuality, and sexual orientation. Raising a teenager is hard in general, but some of these specific issues may affect them differently as young, mixed youth. Youth sometimes struggle with how they feel

about their coloring and how to manage a hair type, whether we straighten our hair or wear it curly. Sexuality may impact girls differently than boys. Be aware of the ways that young girls are sexualized as light-skinned or "exotic." Talk about it.

- Try not to deny one or more of your kids' cultures.
- Recognize the gifts and challenges of a mixed-race experience.
- Form or find a community that speaks to your child's mixed-race experiences.
- Be aware of your own potential prejudice and/or anger about race and racism.
- Recognize that the experiences of mixed-race people are wide and varied.
- When in situations that involve predominantly one race (for instance, family gatherings with people who may not look like your child), recognize that your child may feel isolated.
- Ask questions, ask questions, ask questions.

Be patient and open. In the end, love, attention, and awareness will always win. Parent to parent: stay strong, and enjoy raising your child regardless of his or her racial mix.

CONTRIBUTORS

Montana Baerg: I'm Seneca and Métis, from the Six Nations Reserve. I am a portrait artist and an improvisational actor. I am studying at OCAD University in Toronto, a goal that I had set for myself.

Bianca Craven: I am twenty years old, and I have my own pet-care business. I am an ambitious young woman with dreams galore. I see a future as a businesswoman, a veterinarian, a mom, and a superwoman. Just live it! At the end of the day, think and do for nobody but you.

"Angelina Jones": Colombian, Jamaican, Native, and French background. I am in my last year of high school and will continue my education at George Brown College, in makeup and aesthetics. I carry myself as a young, proud, biracial woman, continuing my dreams and learning life.

Elizabeth Jennifer Hollo: I was born in Toronto. My mother is Grenadian, and my father was Hungarian. I'm twenty now and am just cleaning up the train wreck I call my life: heartbreak, family being ripped apart, friends gone, my father getting sick. In between all of that, I found Karen and this mixed-race group. I walked away each time with something new. One piece of advice: Just be you! Find out who you are. It's a journey.

Spencer Brigham: Ojibwa from Walpole Island and Tohono O'odam from Arizona. I am a multi-instrumental artist with a special interest in classical guitar. I am entering the third year of my Fine Arts degree at York University.

Ocean Windsong: Nuu-chah-nulth/Mik'maq. I was declared Willing Participant/MVP Indigenous Youth Leadership Team Member. After I graduate from high school I plan to work in technical support for the arts.

Jelissa Pamplona: I am half–black Nova Scotian and half-Portuguese, and I can speak Portuguese. I am eighteen years old and am in college, studying to be a social worker. I am in love with hip-hop dancing.

Janine Berridge: Trinidad, Aruba, Saint Vincent. West Indian. Spanish. Black. Indian. White. I am a woman who loves her culture.

Andrew Ernest Brankley: I am of English, Irish, Scottish, French, German, and Guyanese descent. When I submitted my pieces to this book, I was twenty-five. I am thankful for the love and support I have experienced in my life, especially from my mother, a teacher. I'm focusing my efforts on a career in clinical psychology.

Justin Robinson: I was born and raised in Toronto by my beautiful mother of Trinidadian and Venezuelan roots. I'm passionate about basketball, and I coached the team Motion Spirit for the Ontario Basketball Association. I also have a great passion for music.

Chiloh Turner: Hungarian, black, Japanese, Spanish, and Native make me. I'm a bundle of energy and very opinionated. My shoulder's always free to lean on. During my teenage years, I lured myself an agent who landed me some life experience: jobs, a couple music videos, fashion shows ... As I got older, I began to really come into tune with music, writing, producing, visioning, fashion, hosting, and acting.

Kalale Dalton: My dad is "white" from Newfoundland, and my mom is "black" from Uganda. I have had the same e-mail address since I was in fourth grade. I love food and old VHS tapes. I think I'm funny. I have lived in downtown Toronto my whole life. I completed Canada World Youth. I hope this doesn't sound like a personals ad.

Karen Arthurton: I'm of French/Armenian and West Indian background. I have spent a lifetime trying to figure out what being of mixed race means to me, in both my personal and my professional life. I've written a thesis about biraciality, and I have had the privilege of working with the contributors to this book. The label "biracial" is complex, but I would have it no other way!

Alexandre Nahdee: I'm Ojibwa and Portuguese, from Walpole Island First Nation. I am a visual artist, in my third year at OCAD University in Toronto. I am working toward a major in drawing and painting and a minor in Aboriginal studies.

Karuna Sagara: Half–Japanese Canadian. Half–European American. Whole human being. Daughter. Sister. Titi (aunt). Mum (to a Jack Russell/Chihuahua). Lover. Friend. World explorer. Downtown Torontonian. Teacher. Truthseeker. Lovemaker. Soulshaker.

Leslie Kachena McCue: I am a Mississauga Ojibwa from Curve Lake First Nation, and the executive assistant at the Association for Native Development in the Performing and Visual Arts in Toronto. I'm a traditional and jingle-dress dancer, and have performed at the 2010 Winter Olympic Games, the Talking Stick Festival, the REELKids Film Festival, and in Europe.

Natasha Adiyana Morris: I am a storyteller in the Toronto theater community. Cultural perspectives play a role in how I define myself and in the art I create. The delivery of language, movement, spirituality, and political context are rooted in my Canadian-Jamaican-wombanist persona. I am cofounder and artistic director for outreach of AfroChic, a not-for-profit organization that challenges systemic oppression and spearheads community development.

Lalo Lorza: I'm nineteen and was born in Toronto to an Irish Canadian mother and a Colombian father. I have a passion for traveling, history, and culture, and for producing hip-hop instrumentals and writing lyrics. At a young age I became a gang member, but after things fell apart, I decided to try to better my life and others' through music.

Lynnea Jones: I'm a mixed-race nineteen-year-old living in Toronto. I grew up with my mom and never met my father, so I'm aware only of my Native side. It was hard to explain to people that I was mixed, and I asked myself how I could claim to be mixed without knowing what I was mixed with. I decided to tell people I'm full Native, because in my eyes I am.

Yvonne Sanchez-Tieu: Canadian-born. Latino and Southeast Asian background. Culturally urban Torontonian. I am a mixed-race young woman, straddling two different worlds. Passionate to move beyond race and diminish racism, I hope to be a voice for those who are going through the challenges mixed-race people often face. I hope this book will enlighten, inspire, and educate others as it has me.

Mia-Skye Sagara: Born and raised in Toronto. I am the daughter of a Japanese Canadian mother and a British-born Jewish father. I am an emcee, spoken word and visual artist, and the mother of a young daughter. I have performed extensively in Toronto's poetry circuit, and have been showcased in several art shows throughout the city, as well as in the U.S., where I lived for many years, teaching art-based classes to at-risk youth.

An extended thank-you to those we interviewed: Carol Camper, Jacqueline Kalaidjian, Jorge Lozano, Veronica Salvatierra, and Tomás Sebastian. We also thank those who wished to remain anonymous.

ACKNOWLEDGMENTS

First, we would like to thank all the members of the Making Sense of One group, who came together and poured their hearts and souls into this book. Your commitment to this project and your creativity are recognized. Our sincerest thanks to: Bailey Allett, Janine Berridge, Andrew Ernest Brankley, Bianca Craven, Kalale Dalton, Elizabeth Jennifer Hollo, Ialo Iorza, Justin Robinson, Karuna Sagara, Yvonne Sanchez-Tieu, and Chiloh Turner.

Thanks to all the other contributors: Montana Baerg, Spencer Brigham, "Angelina Jones," Lynnea Jones, Leslie Kachena McCue, Natasha Adiyana Morris, Alexandre Nahdee, Jelissa Pamplona, Mia-Skye Sagara, and Ocean Windsong. Your stories enriched this book.

A special thank-you to Andrea Douglas for all her hard work and sensitivity in editing this book, and for effectively capturing the essence of youth voices.

In recognition of all those who agreed to be interviewed, sharing their knowledge and personal stories: Carol Camper, Jacqueline Kalaidjian, Jorge Lorzano, Veronica Salvatierra, and Tomás Sebastian.

An extended thank-you to Bridget Sinclair, Manager of Youth Services, for recognizing the importance of the issues that impact biracial and/or mixed-race youth and for investing her energy, support, and direction in youth members and staff alike. An additional thank-you goes to Eileen Shannon for her support and for connecting our group with Mo-D Productions.

A thank-you to Mo-D Productions, Kevin Barton, and all of their crew for effectively capturing in a phenomenal documentary both the stories of our youth and the creation of this book. This deeply touches our hearts.

A thank-you to the Youth Arcade funders: the City of Toronto Access, Equity and Human Rights (AEHR) Community Partnership and Investment Program, and United Way for supporting this project.

A big thank-you to Annick Press for their commitment to recognizing youth as experts and for journeying with us on this third book.

Last but not least, a sincere thank-you to St. Stephen's Community House (Liane Regendanz, Bill Sinclair, and our dedicated Board of Directors) for their continuing commitment to innovation.

Karen Arthurton
Coordinator, Making Sense of One | St. Stephen's Community House

ABOUT ST. STEPHEN'S COMMUNITY HOUSE AND THE YOUTH ARCADE PROGRAM

St. Stephen's Community House is a unique, community-based social service agency that has been serving the needs of Kensington Market and surrounding neighborhoods in downtown West Toronto since 1962.

Operating with a staff of over 150 people and with the support of almost 400 volunteers, we provide services for more than 32,000 people a year. St. Stephen's addresses the most pressing issues in its community—poverty, hunger, homelessness, unemployment, isolation, conflict and violence, AIDS, racism, youth alienation, and the integration of refugees and immigrants.

Specifically, we will endeavor to maintain and to enhance our role as a leader and partner in the community by providing:
- A quick response to community needs
- Access to a range of services for children, youth, adults, and seniors
- Immigrant and refugee support programs
- Advocacy to improve the quality of life of our community
- Support for community capacity building
- Effective, high impact programs

THE YOUTH ARCADE'S MISSION: To provide a range of youth services that (1) meet emerging and critical youth social, health, recreation, and education needs; (2) empower youth to speak, advocate, and lead youth programming that impacts on their lives; (3) assist youth facing a range of barriers and life experiences through the transition to young adulthood safely and confidently; (4) encourage youth to think critically about themselves and the community in which they live.

How do we make sense of our mission? The Arcade has become the hub of the youth community in our neighborhoods. Youth know it to be a place where they can get information in a non-judgmental and supportive environment. Parents know it's a safe place where their kids can hang out and socialize with their peers while getting information and support. In addition, the Arcade programs are designed to assist youth in making the transition from being teenagers to being young adults. Programs support our youth in their educational endeavors, support their social skills and learning, and help them develop leadership skills and build resilience. Funders know it as a well-managed, youth-driven program with strong community networks. St. Stephen's Community House and the Youth Arcade receive ongoing financial support from the City of Toronto and the United Way of Greater Toronto.

ALSO AVAILABLE FROM ANNICK PRESS

"Passionate, open, and honest ... This book will undoubtedly have more teen appeal than a book on the same subject written by adults."
—*VOYA*

"Excellent book ... sex-ed material that [is] equally positive and empowering ... frank, girl-friendly but never cloying tone."
—*The Globe and Mail*, Toronto

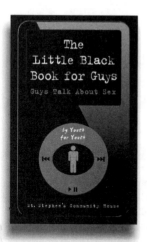

"[The] focus is clearly on the importance of being informed, the value of communicating with and respecting your partner, and staying healthy."
—*VOYA*

"The advice is practical, supportive and non-judgmental. Like the *Little Black Book for Girlz*, [it] will be 'borrowed' or somehow, mysteriously disappear, never to return ... Highly recommended."
—*CM Magazine*